Disney · PIXAR

Cars

MOVIE THEATER
Storybook

Adapted by Cindy Stierle

Contents

Reader's
Digest
Children's Books®

Pleasantville, New York • Montréal, Québec • Bath, United Kingdom

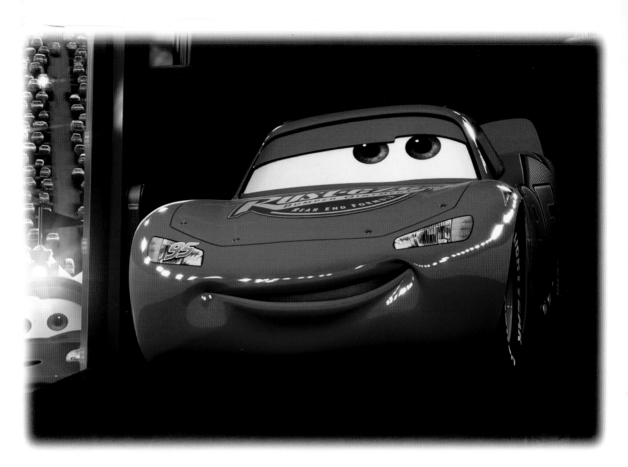

The Rookie

DISK 1
ROUTE
1

The last car race of the season was about to begin. The winner would take home the biggest prize in the racing world—the Piston Cup. Cheers from excited fans echoed through the stadium.

But it was quiet inside the trailer of the hotshot racer Lightning McQueen. "I am speed," he whispered to himself. "I am Lightning."

ROUTE
2

When he finally rolled onto the racetrack, the crowd roared. McQueen could be the first rookie ever to win the Piston Cup.

But winning wouldn't be a cruise down easy street for McQueen. The rookie had to beat The King, who had won more Piston Cups than any other race car. The King was retiring. This was his final race and he wanted to go out on top.

McQueen also had to beat Chick Hicks, who had never won a Piston Cup. Instead, he'd always finished second. Chick was determined to beat The King and McQueen this time— and he didn't mind playing dirty!

For both Chick and McQueen,
there was more at stake than just
the Piston Cup. Since The King
was retiring, the Dinoco Company
would be looking for a new car to
sponsor. Whoever won this race was
sure to be the next face of Dinoco,
which meant fame *and* fortune.
Winning this race meant *everything*.

The cars lined up at the starting line, the flag waved, and they were off! Lap after lap, the three cars battled for the lead. Then McQueen made a bold move, leaving Chick in third place! Chick wasn't about to let McQueen beat him. He knocked the rookie off the track. Next Chick bumped into another car, causing cars to crash all over the track!

ROUTE **8**

DISK 2

ROUTE **9**

"Get through that, McQueen!" Chick called. And that's just what the rookie did. Chick was furious! When Chick and the remaining cars pulled in for a pit stop, McQueen kept going—and took the lead!

Finally, McQueen had to pull in. His crew hustled around him, filling up the tank and getting new tires. "No tires! Just gas!" he told his crew. Then he sped out of pit row without fresh tires.

McQueen's risky move was paying off. With only one lap to go he was in the lead by a full lap! Then—KA-BLAM! KA-BLAM!

McQueen's rear tires blew out. The King and Chick caught up just as McQueen tried to edge across the finish line. The race was too close to call!

Who had won?

While the judges looked at the instant replay, reporters surrounded McQueen and asked him lots of questions.

"I'm a one-man show," said the cocky McQueen. His insulted pit crew quit on the spot!

ROUTE **13** The King tried to offer McQueen some advice. "You ain't gonna win unless you got good folks behind you."

ROUTE **14** But McQueen was too busy dreaming of fame and fortune to hear the good advice The King offered. But he did hear the race results: it was a three-way tie! McQueen was shocked—and embarrassed. He thought he had won. McQueen, The King, and Chick would have a tiebreaking race in California in one week.

Before he could leave, McQueen had to make an appearance for his

sponsor, Rust-eze. His sponsor's tent was filled with old cars. McQueen shuddered as he entered.

"You're my hero, Mr. McQueen," a rusty truck called out.

The rookie race car forced a smile. After he won the race in California, he was sure to get the coveted Dinoco sponsorship and he would drop Rust-eze. McQueen wanted fancy tents and private helicopters, not medicated bumper ointment. To McQueen, nothing mattered except winning next week's race.

Route 66

DISK 1
ROUTE
1

*L*ightning McQueen was determined to reach California first. "We're driving all night," McQueen told Mack, the loyal truck that pulled the trailer he rode in.

But as the night wore on and the miles rolled away, Mack grew sleepy. McQueen promised to stay awake to help the big truck. But he didn't. The race car was sleeping when a group of hot rods swarmed around Mack.

The hot rods decided to play tricks with the sleepy truck. They played some soft music, and then started bumping him.

All of a sudden, one of the hot rods sneezed. Mack awoke with a start. The truck swerved, causing the sleeping McQueen to roll out the back of the trailer!

BEEEP! A horn blared, waking McQueen. The confused race car found himself facing the wrong way on the Interstate. He spun around, trying to find Mack. But since race cars don't have headlights, McQueen couldn't see very well. He followed the wrong trailer off an exit ramp onto an old highway.

Lights flashed behind McQueen. It was a police cruiser. McQueen was actually relieved—until he heard a noise echo across the desert. BANG! BANG!

"Why is he shooting at me?" the race car wondered, terrified. He didn't realize that the noise was actually Sheriff's tailpipe backfiring.

A scared McQueen tore away. He sped into a sleepy town where he got tangled in some wire, knocked down a statue, and ripped up the main street. He wound up dangling between two telephone poles, and then he passed out.

The next morning, McQueen awoke in a locked impound lot with a parking boot on his wheel. A rusty tow truck was peering in at him.

ROUTE 5
"Mornin'," said the happy tow truck. "My name is Mater."

"What? Where am I?" gasped a very confused McQueen.

"You're in Radiator Springs," Mater said proudly, "the cutest little town in Carburetor County."

ROUTE 6
It wasn't long before Sheriff arrived. McQueen was due in court.

McQueen didn't think much of
the run-down town. And the crowd
gathered in the courthouse didn't
think much of McQueen, even if he
was a race car. So when the judge,
Doc Hudson, ordered McQueen to
leave town, no one could believe it!
McQueen was thrilled.

Then Sally, the town attorney,
rolled into the courtroom. The sleek
blue car thought McQueen should
fix the road he ruined. Their little

town couldn't afford to lose any more business.

Overruled by the townsfolk, Doc changed his mind. "You're going to fix the road under my supervision!" sentenced Doc. McQueen would be working with Bessie.

DISK 2

ROUTE
9

ROUTE
10

"Bessie?" the race car wondered, looking at Mater.

Bessie turned out to be the huge road-paving machine that McQueen would have to pull.

McQueen was not going to hang around and fix the road. As soon as Mater took off the parking boot, the race car sped away.

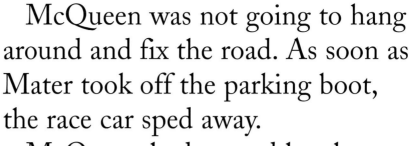 McQueen had a good laugh— until he ran out of gas! Sheriff had emptied McQueen's tank.

ROUTE 14 Reluctantly, McQueen let Mater hook him up to Bessie. But just as he got started, two minivans arrived. "Customers!" Sally shouted.

 ROUTE 15 The shopkeepers tried desperately to sell things to the minivans. But the lost couple just wanted directions.

 ROUTE 16 They left town as fast as they could.

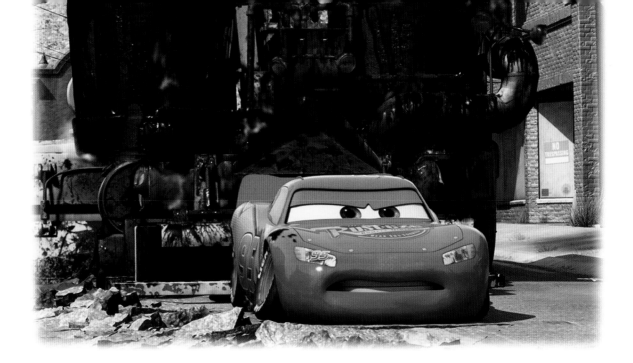

New Friends

The day of the big race was coming, and McQueen was determined to get out of Radiator Springs. He worked fast—and was sloppy.

"It's done," the race car declared.

"It looks awful," Sally said.

"Now it matches the rest of the town," McQueen replied rudely.

Doc was angry. "The deal was you fix the road, not make it worse."

"I'm a race car, not a bulldozer," McQueen shot back.

"Then why don't we have a little race. Me and you," Doc challenged.

DISK 1
ROUTE
1

ROUTE
2

McQueen could leave if he beat Doc. But if he lost, he'd have to do the road over. McQueen smiled. This was his ticket out of town. There was no way old Doc could beat him.

The entire town gathered at a nearby butte to watch. When the race started, McQueen took off but Doc didn't move.

"C'mon, Mater," Doc finally said. "Might need a little help."

It wasn't Doc that needed help. McQueen skidded on a sharp turn and landed in a cactus patch.

"You drive like you fix roads," Doc called to the rookie. "Lousy."

Mater laughed as he pulled McQueen out. "I'm startin' to think he knowed you was gonna crash."

McQueen went back to town and scraped up the road. He worked all night repaving one section of it.

ROUTE
8

In the morning, the townsfolk couldn't believe their eyes. McQueen had done a great job! But the race car was nowhere in sight.

DISK 2
ROUTE
9

Doc found McQueen back out at yesterday's racing sight. He was practicing the turn he had missed.

But he couldn't seem to get it right.
  "Turn right to go left," Doc advised the rookie. McQueen scoffed at the advice. What did Doc know about racing?

  After Doc left, McQueen tried it, and missed the turn again. So he returned to town to finish paving.

  The race car continued doing such a good job that the rest of the town started fixing up their shops, too. Now everyone wanted the whole town to look good!

At the end of the day, McQueen was dusty and dirty from all his hard work when he got a cold surprise. Red, the fire engine, gave him a wash. Then Sally, who owned the local motel, invited McQueen to stay in one of her rooms instead of at the impound lot.

She wanted to thank McQueen for his hard work. Sally was starting to like McQueen…and McQueen was starting to like her, too.

Later that night, Mater said to McQueen, "I know something we can do." He and McQueen sneaked to a field and went tractor tipping.

The friends crept quietly toward a tractor, and honked their horns. BEEP! The tractors slowly fell over. The race car was surprised. He was

actually having fun—until an angry harvester named Frank showed up.

"Run!" laughed Mater, as they made a quick escape.

On the way back to town, Mater showed off his backward driving. McQueen was impressed. He didn't have mirrors, so he had never driven backwards. Then he told Mater all about the big race he was going to win. "We're talking a big sponsor with private helicopters," McQueen bragged. The rookie promised that if he won, he'd get Mater a ride in a helicopter.

"I knowed I made a good choice," Mater said.

"In what?" asked McQueen.

"My best friend," answered the happy tow truck.

McQueen felt happier than he'd felt in a long time. But as he drove into his room at the motel, he was stopped by Sally. She'd overheard his promise to Mater.

"Did you mean it?" Sally asked. "Mater trusts you," she added.

McQueen had never really thought about keeping promises.

The two cars said good night. As McQueen watched Sally go, he had a lot to think about.

A Legend

Early the next morning McQueen needed gas before he started work. When he found Sheriff at Doc's clinic, Doc shooed him away. Upset, McQueen kicked a can. CRASH! It landed in Doc's back garage. Curious, McQueen went inside. He saw a lot of junk…and three Piston Cups.

Doc had been a champion race car! Back then he had been known as the Hudson Hornet. McQueen couldn't believe it.

Doc wasn't happy that McQueen had stumbled on his secret.

DISK 1
ROUTE
1

"You're the Hudson Hornet!" gushed McQueen. "You still hold the record for the most wins in a single season!"

"All I see is a bunch of empty cups," Doc snapped.

"But..." McQueen began, as Doc rolled toward him.

BAM! Doc slammed the garage door in McQueen's face.

McQueen raced off to find the other townsfolk. He told them that Doc was a famous race car. But none of them believed it.

Then Sally arrived. She gave McQueen a full tank of gas— and invited him for a drive.

"Don't you big city cars ever just go for a drive?" she asked him.

"Well, no," the surprised McQueen answered. The race car could have skipped town. But instead he followed Sally through the beautiful countryside to a stop overlooking a huge valley.

McQueen learned that Sally had been a big city attorney. But she'd been unhappy until she found Radiator Springs. "I fell in love," she told McQueen. The little town became her new home.

In the distance, McQueen could see the busy Interstate not far away. The cars on the Interstate didn't even know the town was there. "They're missing it!" he exclaimed.

 Sally told him that the old, winding highway had once been the main road of Radiator Springs. "Back then, cars didn't drive on it to *make* great time. They drove on it to *have* a great time. Then the town got bypassed just to save ten minutes of driving."

When they got back to the town, McQueen thanked Sally. "It's kind of nice to slow down every once in a while," he said.

DISK 2
ROUTE
9

Suddenly, a stampede of escaped tractors stumbled through town. McQueen offered to help round them up. He followed a tractor out to the butte and found Doc wearing his racing tires. McQueen watched in awe as Doc sped around the track at top speed!

"Wow! You're amazing," McQueen told Doc.

Doc didn't know McQueen had been watching him. He glared at the rookie and sped away.

But McQueen wasn't going to let it go. He followed Doc back to the garage. "How could a car like you quit at the top of your game?"

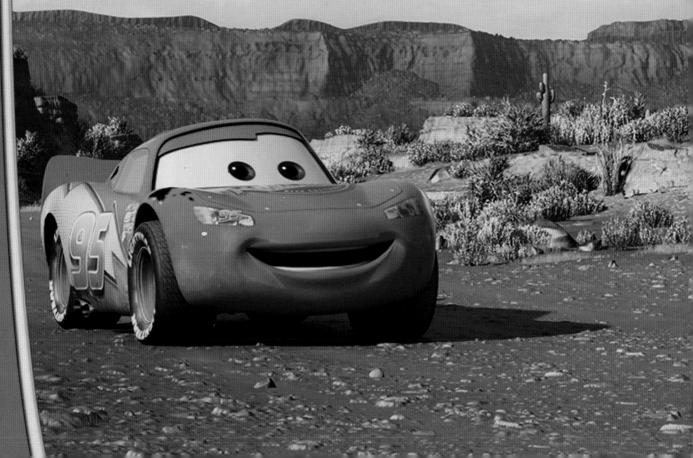

"They quit on me!" Doc snapped. Doc had been injured in a car wreck. He recovered, but when he returned, the racing world had forgotten about him. He had been replaced by a hotshot rookie just like McQueen.

"Just finish that road and get outta here," Doc told McQueen.

Once again, McQueen worked all night. In the morning, the road was finished. And that meant McQueen could leave.

"Good riddance," Doc said.

But McQueen didn't leave. Instead, he decided to help out all of his new friends. He became the best customer the town had seen in a long time.

 He got new whitewall tires, tried organic fuel, bought night-vision goggles and bumper stickers, and even got a new paint job!

And that night, McQueen had a special surprise for Sally.

 At McQueen's signal, all the shopkeepers turned on their neon lights. The town was lit up for the first time in years!

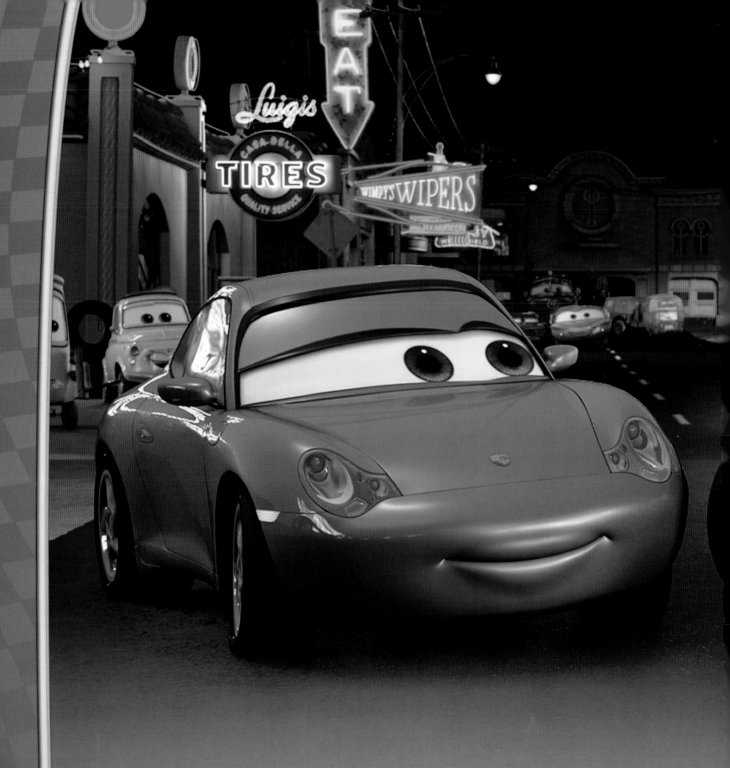

The cars cruised up and down the newly paved street. McQueen was happier than he'd ever been before. He looked at Sally, wanting to tell her how he felt.

Suddenly, a spotlight shone on McQueen. The world had found the missing race car!

"I'm sorry I lost you, Boss," Mack called, as he rounded the corner. With him came a flood of reporters. They surrounded McQueen, pushing Sally out of the way.

McQueen had to leave right away to make it to the race on time. But the race car wasn't sure how to say good-bye.

McQueen found Sally, but he was speechless.

"I hope you find what you're looking for," she said sadly and disappeared into the crowd.

As the reporters pressed in, McQueen backed into his trailer to escape. Mack quickly closed the trailer and pulled out of town. So did the reporters, though one stopped to thank Doc for tipping them off to McQueen's location.

Sally was stunned. Doc tried to explain. "It was best for everyone."

"Best for everyone? Or best for you?" she asked Doc.

The rest of the town was quiet.

"I didn't even get to say good-bye," Mater said sadly. Everyone went home and turned off their lights. The hope that McQueen had brought to the town had left with him.

Doc remained alone, in the center of town, with Sally's words running through his head.

The Big Race

DISK 1
ROUTE
1

nce again, fans filled the stadium with cheers, this time at the big Los Angeles racetrack. McQueen was in the biggest race of his life! But this time winning didn't seem all that important to him anymore.

Chick and The King were far ahead. McQueen was so busy thinking about Sally and Radiator Springs that he almost hit a wall!

ROUTE
2

ROUTE
3

Suddenly, McQueen heard a voice over his radio. It was Doc! "I knew you needed a crew chief," Doc said, "but I didn't know it was this bad."

The announcers couldn't believe it. The famous Hudson Hornet was Lightning McQueen's crew chief!

And Doc had pulled a crew together from Radiator Springs.

"You can win this race with your eyes shut," Doc said.

ROUTE 4

ROUTE 5

42

Inspired, the rookie poured on the speed. Chick tried to bump McQueen off the track. But McQueen used the backward driving he'd learned from Mater to stay on track. When Chick bumped him again he used Doc's turn-right-to-go-left trick and took the lead. With help from his great pit crew, it looked as if McQueen would win!

Then McQueen saw that Chick had caused The King to crash.

DISK 2

McQueen stopped right before the finish line. This was no way for The King to end his career.

As Chick raced past, McQueen turned around and pushed The King across the finish line.

Chick had finally won a Piston Cup—and the fans booed him!

But the crowd cheered for The King and McQueen—the rookie that knew what winning really meant.

Tex, the owner of Dinoco, was so impressed that he offered McQueen the Dinoco sponsorship. But McQueen was staying loyal to Rust-eze, his original sponsors that had given him his big break.

McQueen did ask for one favor from Dinoco, though…

A short time later, Sally was back in the mountains that overlooked the town. Suddenly, she heard a voice say, "There's a rumor floating around that some hotshot Piston Cup race car is setting up his big racing headquarters here."

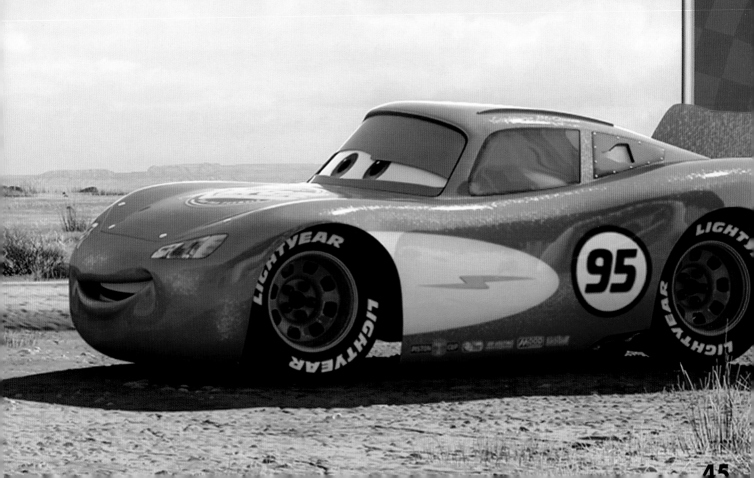

The two cars smiled at each other. McQueen was finally ready to tell Sally how he felt…

…when Mater flew by in a Dinoco helicopter. McQueen laughed. And McQueen knew that he and Sally would have plenty of time together.

Because McQueen had found his home—and himself—in Radiator Springs.